DR. NINTH

originated by Roger Hargreaves

Written and illustrated by Adam Hargreaves

It was a lovely sunny day, and the Doctor decided to go shopping in town.

The first shop he came to was a clothes shop.

"Good morning," said the Doctor.

"Hello, my name is Rose," said the woman who worked in the shop. "How can I help you?"

"I was thinking about buying a hat," replied the Doctor. "I like the look of that one."

He pointed to one of the shop mannequins.

"Although, there is something rather familiar about it . . ."

"I'm not sure that one really suits you," said Rose.

As she turned to show the Doctor some other hats, the mannequin suddenly moved its head.

And then, without warning, it tried to grab Rose.

Luckily the Doctor grabbed her first as all the other mannequins came to life.

"We've got to escape!" exclaimed the Doctor, pulling Rose out to the street.

"But what's going on?" cried Rose.

"They've turned into Autons!" cried the Doctor, running into Mr. Socket's electrical shop next door as the mannequins chased them.

The Doctor used his sonic screwdriver to switch on all the machines in the electrical shop.

"That should distract them for a moment," said the Doctor.

The whirling blenders and popping toasters and tumbling tumble dryers gave the Doctor and Rose time to escape from the electrical shop and into Miss Dinky's toy shop.

"How is this happening?" asked Rose.

"Autons do not act on their own. The Nestene Consciousness brought the mannequins to life. They can animate any plastic object," explained the Doctor. "They must have a transmitter somewhere, and that is what we need to find to stop them."

"It's a shame they can't bring other things to life. Like a jam tart. A jam tart wouldn't be so scary!" said Rose.

Rose peered anxiously out of the window.

"Oh no!" she cried. "The Autons have caught someone!"

"That's not just someone," said the Doctor. "That's my friend Jack. Quick, we have to help him!"

With a wave of his sonic screwdriver, the Doctor activated all the toys in the shop.

The toys raced out of the shop, and under the control of the Doctor's sonic, they freed Jack.

"That's a very handy toy," said Rose.

"This is *not* a toy," said the Doctor. "This is a sonic screwdriver."

"Rose, I'd like you to meet Captain Jack Harkness. Jack, this is Rose," said the Doctor.

"Nice to meet you, Rose," said Jack. "Doctor, I think the Auton transmitter is up on that roof."

Jack pointed to the roof above Mrs. Sprout's Greengrocer's, where they could see more Autons looking down at them.

"What we need are cabbages," announced the Doctor.

"Cabbages?" said Rose with a puzzled look.

"Yes, cabbages, and lots of them," added the Doctor.

So the three of them grabbed as many of Mrs. Sprout's cabbages as they could carry and climbed up the fire escape to the roof.

On the roof, they found a group of Autons guarding the control device.

"How's your aim?" asked the Doctor, and then he threw a cabbage.

It sailed through the air and hit an Auton square on the head, knocking it clean off.

"Remember, they are only mannequins!" cried the Doctor.

Rose threw a cabbage and knocked another head off.

"Fantastic!" the Doctor said with a grin.

In no time at all, the Doctor and Rose and Jack had knocked off the heads of all the Autons.

And then the Doctor disabled the Auton transmitter.

With a cabbage!

"What a mess," sighed Rose. "How am I ever going to get the shop straightened out?"

"What are you saying?" exclaimed the Doctor. "Here we are, just saved the whole world, and you're worrying about a shop!"

"Couldn't you just wave your sonic thingamajig and clean this all up?"

"It is *not* a magic wand," said the Doctor. "Now, I think we all deserve a cup of tea back in the TARDIS."

"What is the TARDIS?" asked Rose.

"You will have to wait and see," the Doctor said, grinning.

Rose was amazed by the TARDIS, or rather she was amazed once she entered it.

"How is it bigger on the inside?" she exclaimed.

"Ah, that's my little secret," answered the Doctor.

"Something I like to keep under my hat!"

Rose laughed. "If you had bought one, that is!"